YOUNG READERS EDITION

STEVEN SPIELBERG'S

E.T.

THE EXTRA-TERRESTRIAL
STORYBOOK

Other books by William Kotzwinkle

ELEPHANT BANGS TRAIN
HERMES 3000
NIGHTBOOK
THE FAN MAN
SWIMMER IN THE SECRET SEA
DR. RAT
FATA MORGANA
HERR NIGHTINGALE AND THE SATIN WOMAN
JACK IN THE BOX
E.T. THE EXTRA-TERRESTRIAL
E.T. THE EXTRA-TERRESTRIAL STORYBOOK
E.T. THE BOOK OF THE GREEN PLANET
E.T. THE STORYBOOK OF THE GREEN PLANET
CHRISTMAS AT FONTAINE'S
GREAT WORLD CIRCUS
QUEEN OF SWORDS
SEDUCTION IN BERLIN

YOUNG READERS EDITION

STEVEN SPIELBERG'S

E.T.

THE EXTRA-TERRESTRIAL STORYBOOK

by
WILLIAM KOTZWINKLE
based on a screenplay by
MELISSA MATHISON

BERKLEY BOOKS, NEW YORK

E.T.
THE EXTRA-TERRESTRIAL STORYBOOK

A Berkley Book / published by arrangement with
MCA Publishing Rights, a Division of MCA INC.

PRINTING HISTORY
Berkley Young Reader's edition / October 1988

ISBN: 0-425-11559-3

A BERKLEY BOOK ® TM 757-375
Berkley Books are published by The Berkley Publishing Group,
200 Madison Avenue, New York, New York 10016.
The name "BERKLEY" and the "B" logo are
trademarks belonging to Berkley Publishing Corporation.
PRINTED IN THE UNITED STATES OF AMERICA

10 9 8 7 6 5 4 3 2 1

The spaceship floated gently, anchored by a beam of lavender light to the earth below. Round in shape and glowing warmly, it looked like a gigantic old Christmas tree ornament fallen from the night sky. The Ship landed on Earth purposefully, the intelligence commanding it beyond navigational error. Yet an error was about to be made . . .

The hatch was open, the crew out and about, probing the earth with strangely shaped tools, like little old elves caring for their misty, moonlit gardens. It was clear they weren't elves, but creatures more scientifically minded. For they were taking samples —of flowers, moss, shrubs, saplings. Yet their misshapen heads, their drooping arms and roly-poly, sawed-off torsos would make one think of elfland, and the tenderness they showed the plants might add to this impression—were someone of Earth nearby to observe it, but no one was, and the elfin botanists from space were free to work in peace.

Even so, they started in fear when a bat twittered by, or an owl hooted, or a dog barked in the distance. Then their breathing quickened and a mistlike camouflage surrounded them, flowing from their fingertips and from their long toes.

Nothing could camouflage their Ship, however, and it had already been detected by military radar and other scanning devices. Government specialists in extraterrestrial research were bouncing around the back roads in noisy vehicles, talking to each other on radios, closing in on the great ornament.

But the little old crew of botanists were not really disturbed as they carried their prizes from Earth's soil up the hatchway and into the immense greenhouse that was the core of the ship. They knew that they had plenty of time to escape before the Earthmen reached them.

The little crew of botanists had collected one of everything that grew or had grown on Earth throughout its existence—or nearly one of everything, since their work was not yet done. Were an expert from one of Earth's great botanical gardens to come into this greenhouse, he would find plants he'd never seen before except in fossil form, imprinted in coal.

An extraterrestrial botanist left the greenhouse after planting an herb he had dug up and went down the glowing hatchway into the night air, his body exhaling faint mist as he searched for more plants. When he passed a colleague, their eyes did not meet. But something else took place; their chests glowed simultaneously, an inner, red glow from the heart region suffusing their thin, translucent skin.

Mist-shrouded, the botanist entered grass as high as his head and came out at the edge of a redwood forest. His naturally distended stomach skimmed the forest floor. Though he looked like a goblin, he had a body that was suitably arranged to give him a low and stable center of gravity. However, it was not a form that Earth folks could readily take to, these large webbed feet coming almost directly out of his low-hanging belly and his long hands trailing along ape-fashion beside it. As he moved quietly through the forest, knuckles brushing the leaves, he searched the dark forest with enormous bulbous eyes—the kind of eyes you might find on a giant frog hopping along.

Through millions of years' experience, this botanist and his colleagues had remained shy and had never had the inclination to make contact with anything other than plant life on Earth. A failing perhaps, but they'd monitored things long enough to know that to Earthmen, their beautiful ship was first of all a target and they themselves material for a taxidermist to display under glass. Why would they want to instruct humans with their vast knowledge when they would only be laughed at because their noses were like bashed-in Brussels sprouts and their general appearance like that of overgrown prickly pears?

The botanist paused at a little redwood sapling, examined it carefully, then dug it out, murmuring to it in his gravelly space tongue, words of weird, unearthly shape; but the redwood seemed to understand.

A sea of yellow house lights glowed tantalizingly

from a little suburb in a valley beyond the trees. The botanist had been curious about those houses for some time, and tonight would be the last night he could investigate them. His Ship would leave Earth for an extended period, until the next great mutation in Earth vegetation, a period marked by centuries. It would be the last chance he'd have to peek in the windows. On the long voyage back through space, he'd entertain his shipmates with accounts of what he saw. The ancient crinkle lines at his eyes smiled.

He tiptoed down the edge of the fire road on his great webbed feet with great long toes. These feet were fine on his own planet, but they were not ideal on Earth. Where he had come from, things were more fluid, and you could sort of paddle along and only infrequently have to waddle on solid ground.

Then he received a warning signal to return to the Ship, but he decided it was too soon, a warning for those not as fast on their feet as he. His heart-light glowed ruby red in response to the house lights flickering ahead. He loved Earth, especially its plant life, but he liked humanity too, and always, when his heart-light glowed, he wanted to teach them, guide them, give them the stored intelligence of millions of years. But what was the use in trying to teach people who would only laugh at your pear-shaped silhouette?

The ship's warning signal came on again, thumping in his heart-light: the code alarm—all crew return! Danger, danger, danger! His heart-light flashed wildly.

Down the road, shafts of light appeared and grew larger as they raced toward him. A snarling sound became a roaring. He stumbled backward, then sideways, confused by the advancing lights of racing vehicles. It was blinding now, harsh Earth light, cold and clear. He stumbled again and fell off the fire road.

Time, time, time, called the Ship, rounding up its last straggling members.

The vehicles were scattered, as were the drivers. He turned on his protective mist and glided across the road in the moonlight, blending with the foul exhaust from their engines, the noxious cloud momentarily adding to his camouflage, and then he was across the road and sliding down a low ravine. He huddled against the sand and rock, as the Earthmen leapt across the ravine.

He scampered up after the last one had passed and entered the forest behind them. His heart-light grew brighter, the energy field of his group strengthening it as he heard them, all their hearts calling to him, as well as the hundred million years of plant life on board, calling *danger, danger, danger.*

He rushed between the sweeping lights, along the single clear path in the forest, his long toe-roots feeling each impression. Each tangle of leaves, each spiderweb was known to him. He felt their gentle messages, speeding him through the forest, saying *this way, this way . . .*

The extraterrestrial ran, through the forest to the clearing. The Grand Ornament, Jewel of the Galaxy, waited for him. He waddled toward it, toward its serene and beautiful light, light of ten million lights. He pushed along through the grass, trying to become visible to the Ship, to put his heart-light in touch, but his long, ridiculous toes were entangled in some weeds that wouldn't let go.

He yanked loose and pushed forward, into the outermost aura of shiplight, just at the edge of the grass. He spied the hatch, still open, and a crewmate standing in it, heart-light flashing, calling to him, desperately searching.

I'm coming, I'm coming . . .

He shuffled through the grass, but his hanging stomach, shaped by other degrees of gravity, slowed him, and a sudden group decision flooded him, a feeling that swept through his very bones.

The hatch closed, petals folding inward. The Ship lifted off as he burst from the grass, waving his long-fingered hand. But the Ship couldn't see him now. It hovered momentarily, then departed, spinning above the treetops.

The creature stood in the grass, his heart-light flashing with fear.

He was alone, three million light-years from home.

Mary sat in her bedroom, feet up, half reading, half listening to the voices of her two sons and their friends, playing Dungeons & Dragons in the kitchen below.

"So you get to the edge of the forest, but you make a truly stupid mistake, so I'm calling in the Wandering Monsters."

Wandering Monsters, thought Mary. How about suffering mothers like herself? Divorced and living in a house with children who speak a foreign tongue.

"Can I get Wandering Monsters called out for just befriending a goblin?"

Mary sighed. Goblins, mercenaries, orks, you name it, she had it down in her kitchen night after night, as well as the rubble of a ruined city of Crush bottles, potato chip bags, books, papers, calculators.

"Steve's Dungeon Master. He's got Absolute Power."

Absolute Power. But she couldn't even get them to dry a dish. She heard Elliott, her younger son, shouting. "I run down the road. They're after me. Just when they're about to get me and they're really mad, I throw down my portable hole. I climb in and pull the lid closed. Presto. Disappeared into thin air."

Portable hole? If only I had one to disappear into, Mary thought. What had become of her life? Where was the excitement? Where was the romance?

He was waddling down the fire road. The road was silent now, his pursuers gone, but he could not last long in this atmosphere. Earth gravity would get to him, and the ground resistance twist his spine out of shape. The bizarre houseforms of Earth were directly ahead, held down by gravity, unlike the lovely terraces of—but he must not think about home.

Directly ahead of him was a fence. He climbed like a vine to the top, but toppled down the other side, stomach upward, feet flailing. He hit, limbs splaying in every direction, a whimper of pain on his lips, and rolled, pumpkinlike, across the lawn.

What am I doing here, I must be mad . . .

Something in the yard was sending soft signals. He turned and saw the vegetable garden. He crept toward it, embraced an artichoke, and asked the vegetables what he should do. Their advice, to go and look in the kitchen window, was not welcome. I'm already in trouble, he signaled back, because of wanting to peek in windows. The artichoke insisted, grunting softly, and the extraterrestrial crept off obediently. The square of kitchen light radiated outward, ominous as any black hole in space.

At a table in the middle of the room sat five Earthlings, engaged in ritual. The creatures were shouting, and moving tiny idols around on the table. Sheets of paper were waved, bearing dark secrets, for each Earthling kept hidden from the other what was printed there. Then a powerful cube was rattled and tossed, and they all watched its six-sided form land, just so. Again they shouted, consulted their tablets, and moved their idols, as their alien tongues sounded in the night air.

He sank down from the window into darkness again. The planet was unspeakably strange. He was ten million years old and had been a great many places, but he'd never encountered anything as complicated as this. Overwhelmed, he crept away, needing to rest his brain in the vegetable patch. He slumped down next to a cabbage and lowered his head. It was all over. Let them come in the morning, take him away, and stuff him.

The lights of the Pizza Wagon suddenly swept the yard and the extraterrestrial panicked. There's nothing to fear, said a tomato plant. It's only the Pizza Wagon.

The wagon stopped in front of the house. A door in the house opened and he saw an Earthling emerge. That's Elliott, said the green beans. He lives here. The Earthling was near, looking his way. Quickly he covered his heart-light and dove into the toolshed, where he crouched, fearful mist surrounding him. He'd trapped himself, but there were tools in the shed, a digging fork with which to defend himself.

Don't stab yourself in the foot, said a little potted ivy.

From the garden he felt the mental wave of a nearby orange tree, as one of its fruits was plucked by the Earth child. A moment later the fruit hurtled into the toolshed, and struck him in the chest. How humiliating, a botanist of his stature, pelted with ripe fruit. Angrily he grabbed the orange, wound up one of his long, powerful arms, and whipped it back into the night. The Earthling cried out, and scampered away.

"Help! Mom! Help!"

Mary chilled all over.

"There's something out there!" shouted Elliott. "In the toolshed. It threw an orange at me."

"Oooooo," mocked Tyler the Dungeon Master, "sounds dangerous."

Mary grabbed a flashlight and they all headed outdoors. "What exactly did you see?" she asked Elliott.

"In there." He pointed to the toolshed.

Her older boy Michael shouted across the lawn. "The gate's open. Look at these tracks!"

The extraterrestrial could see their forms clearly now from his hiding place. There were the five Earth children . . . and who was that exotic creature with them? His heart-light began to glow, and he quickly covered it over. Deftly, he waddled closer to see more of this tall, willowy being who accompanied the children. The clang-banging syllables of her language were meaningless to him, but he sensed that she was mother to this crew.

As Mary passed under the porch light, and the extraterrestrial gazed at her from his hiding place, thoughts of escape were temporarily put aside. Foolish heart-light, he said to that peculiar organ.

The Earthlings went back into the kitchen, and after a time, three of the Earth children left. The lights went out and the house was quiet.

The extraterrestrial waddled across the yard to have another strategy meeting with the vegetables. But his large foot depressed the hidden edge of a metal garden tool and its handle rose up toward him at a high rate of speed. It struck him in the head and he fell backward with an intergalactic scream, then dashed into the little patch of corn nearby.

Moments later, the back door opened and an Earthling rushed out, with the cowering dog. Elliott charged across the yard, flashlight on. The extraterrestrial lay crouched, trembling all over. The cornstalks separated, the boy looked in, screamed, and dove to the earth.

The space creature backed off through the cornstalks and hurried for the gate, big feet flapping.

"Don't go!"

The boy's voice had an edge of gentleness in it, as young plants have—and the old botanist turned to look at him. Their eyes met.

"Don't go!"

But the ancient being was already going, out the gate and into the night.

"It was here, right here . . ."

The extraterrestrial listened to the voices of the men, who still paced back and forth upon the landing site.

". . . and it slipped through my fingers." The leader, wearing a jingling ring of teeth from his belt, turned. Then he entered his vehicle and they all departed.

The extraterrestrial stared mournfully at the traces the Ship had left. He raised a hand limply. Exhaustion had set in on him, and hunger. The powerful ration tablets he and his crewmates survived on were not of Earth. Oh, for one tiny ration tablet loaded with energy. He slouched back weak, depressed. The end was near, he was sure. But then he heard a sound in the clearing.

The extraterrestrial looked out and saw the Earth child Elliott standing there. The old space being in the nearby bushes did not reveal his presence. It was best to remain unnoticed. An extraterrestrial was about to expire in the underbrush and there was no point in involving strangers.

The boy brought a bag from his pocket, from which he took a tiny object. He placed the object on the ground, walked a few paces, placed another, and another, until he was out of sight, far along a hidden path. The ancient traveler crawled from the bushes and went to see what the Earth child had left there. It was a small round pill, bearing a remarkable resemblance to a space-nutrition tablet. He turned it over in his palm. Upon it was printed an indecipherable code:

M&M

He put it in his mouth to let it dissolve. Delicious. He'd never tasted anything like it anywhere in the galaxy. He hurried along the trail, eating one pill after another, strength returning, hope surging in his heart. The trail led him to the boy's house once more.

He tiptoed across the backyard. To his surprise he found the boy asleep in a sack beside the vegetables. The extraterrestrial shivered and mist poured out of his toes, mists of worry, fear, confusion.

Suddenly the boy's eyes opened. Elliott looked up into enormous eyes, eyes like moon jellyfish with faint tentacles of power within them, eyes charged with ancient and terrible knowledge.

The extraterrestrial stared down, horrified by the boy's protruding nose and large, exposed ears, and worst of all, by his tiny little eyes, dark and beady as those of a coconut.

But the child blinked, and the terror in them touched the old scientist's heart. He extended a long finger and touched the boy's forehead.

Elliott shrieked and scrambled backward, clutching his sleeping bag around him. The extraterrestrial jumped in the other direction. Then he held out his hand and opened it. Within the huge scaly palm was his last M&M, melting.

Elliott looked down at the little candy, then looked up at the monster. The monster pointed a long finger into his palm, then pointed to his mouth.

"Okay," said Elliott softly. He opened his jacket and took out his bag of M&Ms, and backed slowly away, continuing to lay a trail across the yard.

The elderly space traveler followed, picking up each M&M and swallowing it down hungrily. Chocolate dribbled from the corners of his mouth. His fingers were coated with it too. He licked it off deliriously, his strength returning, and before he knew it he had followed the trail into the Earthling's house, up a flight of stairs and down the hallway to the boy's room. There the child rewarded him with a handful of M&Ms. He devoured them in one gulp. It seemed a rash act, but who knew what tomorrow would bring?

The boy's voicebox sounded. "I'm Elliott."

The words were a jumble, incomprehensible. But anyone who would share their M&Ms could be trusted. The extraterrestrial sank down on the floor, exhausted. A blanket came around him and he slept.

The extraterrestrial woke next morning, not knowing what planet he was on.

"Come on, you have to hide." The space creature was pushed across the room into a closet and shut in behind its louvered door. He huddled in the closet as the mother entered and spoke.

"Time for school, Elliott."

"I'm sick, Mom . . ."

The extraterrestrial peeked through the louvers of the closet door. The boy had returned to bed and seemed to plead with the tall, willowy creature. She placed a tube in the boy's mouth and left the room. The boy quickly held it to the light above his bed, heated the fluid within it, and placed it back in his mouth as the mother returned.

"You have a temperature."

"I guess I do."

"Think you'll live if I go to work? Okay," she

went on, "you can stay home. But no TV, understand? You are not to disintegrate in front of the box."

She turned, went through the doorway and down to breakfast. Soon Elliott could hear her out in the driveway where Michael was practicing driving, backing the car toward the street.

"Here you go, Mom," he said, stepping out.

Elliott got out of bed and opened the closet door. The extraterrestrial shrank back. "Hey, come on outta there," said Elliott, extending his hand. Reluctantly, the old monstrosity waddled forward, out of the closet, and looked around.

"What am I gonna call you?" Elliott looked into the great flashing eyes of the monster. "You're an extraterrestrial, right? We'll call you E.T., short for extraterrestrial. Okay?"

The monster came forward. "Do you talk?" Elliott snapped his fingertips up and down like a yakking mouth. E.T. blinked, then moved his own fingertips, making galactic-intelligence patterns, the cosmic super-codes of survival, ten million years' worth.

Elliott walked over to the radio and turned it on. "You like this tune? You like rock 'n' roll?" A sound such as E.T. had never heard before was pouring out of the radio. He covered his sensitive ear-flaps with both hands and crouched low.

Elliott fished a quarter out of his bank. "Here, see—it's a quarter." The object offered was small, flat, round, with a shiny coating, different-hued from the M&M, but possibly this was even stronger survival food. He bit down. A piece of junk.

"Yeah, right," said Elliott, "you can't eat that.

Hey, are you hungry again? I'm hungry. Let's go have something to eat."

E.T. followed Elliott downstairs to the kitchen where Elliott opened drawers, taking out the ingredients of his favorite breakfast. "Waffles," he said, and started stirring up some batter.

E.T. watched as peculiar items appeared, none related to space travel. He picked up a fork. Click, click, click. Four tines, sounding click, click, click. E.T. stared at the fork.

"What's the matter? You make me feel so sad all of a sudden." Elliott's whole body swayed, caught in the high, powerful wave that had spilled over him; emotions he couldn't comprehend filled him up to the brim, as if he'd lost something incredibly wonderful that should have been his, always.

Click, click, click . . . The aged creature had his own eyes closed in contemplation of the heights. Might there be an ear, immense distances away, listening to the song of four tines? But how?

"We're going to have fun," said Elliott, shaking off the sadness and taking hold of the old monster's hand. "Come on . . ."

The long, rootlike fingers entwined with his, and Elliott felt he was leading a child younger than himself, but then the rippling wave washed over him again, bearing star-secrets and cosmic law, and he knew the creature was older than he was, by a great deal. Something altered inside Elliott, turning just slightly; he blinked, amazed at the feeling, the feeling that he was a child of the stars too, and had never done anything to hurt anybody, ever.

He led the waddling E.T. back to the staircase and

up to the bedroom. Elliott opened the closet door and addressed the monster. "We've got to fix you a place in the closet. Make it like the space shuttle, okay? With everything you need."

E.T. was staring up at the skylight of the room with soft shafts of sunlight shining through it. Elliott began arranging the closet with pillows and blankets. He had not stopped to ask himself why he was harboring the monster, or what it meant. He knew this thing had been handed to him from the stars, and he had to follow or—or die.

"You'll like it in here," he called through the door, as he lined up a number of stuffed animals at the mouth of the closet. "That's protective camouflage. You stay in line with them, nobody'll know the difference."

A bewildered E.T. stared dumbly at the arrangements. Elliott stepped forward with a desk lamp. "Light. See?" He switched it on and the harsh glare of its crude interior assaulted E.T.'s eyes. He backed up, into a record player, his arm scraping the needle across the record. In spite of the unpleasant scratching sound, soft lights went off inside him, and again he was filled with developing blueprints for escape —using a fork, and—and something that turns, like this thing I've just bumped into. It will turn, and it will scratch . . . a message . . . He stumbled around, looking for other bits of hardware. He opened the desk drawer, tumbled its contents on his feet.

"Hey," said Elliott, "take it easy. I'm supposed to keep this place neat." He put his hand to the old monster's elbow and led him gently toward the closet. "You stay in there, okay? Stay . . ."

E.T. shuffled into the little enclosure. He who had once supervised the plant life in the grandest mansions of space was being closeted with a skateboard. He slumped down. Where was his Ship, the Wonder of the Universe, now that he needed her?

The closet door shut. E.T. squinted at the harsh light from the lamp, then took a handkerchief from the closet shelf and placed it over the lampshade. It glowed like the light of the Mother Ship. He must signal it, must let his crewmates know that he lived. The image of the fork came into his brain again, four tines trailing in a circle, click, click, click.

"Michael!"

"How you doin', faker . . ." Michael pushed on past Elliott.

"I've got something really important to tell you."

Michael hesitated. "Well, make it fast."

Elliott led Michael over to the closet. "Close your eyes."

"Why?"

"Just do it, will you, Michael?"

Within the closet, Elliott put his arm around E.T. and nodded reassuringly. "Come on, meet my brother." They stepped out, just as Gertie, home from nursery school, raced into the room. Seeing the monster, she screamed, as did the monster, and Michael who'd just opened his eyes.

"Elliott, we've got to tell Mom."

"We can't, Michael. She'll want to do the right

thing. You know what that means, don't you?"
Elliott pointed at E.T. "He'll wind up as dog food."

Harvey thumped his tail.

"Does he talk?"

"No."

"Well, what is he doing here?"

"I don't know."

The two boys looked at their five-year-old sister,
who was staring at the creature, her eyes wide.

"Gertie, he won't hurt you. You can touch him."

The stranded old traveler submitted to more probing and prodding, the children's fingertips pulsing
their messages inward to his deep receptors, and
though the message was chaotic and confused, these
little coconuts weren't stupid. But could they lift
him into the Great Nebula?

"You're not going to tell, are you, Gertie? Not
even Mom?"

"Why not?"

"Because—grownups can't see him. Only kids see
him."

"I don't believe you."

Elliott took Gertie's doll from her hands. "You
know what will happen if you tell? Promise not to
tell?"

"Is he from the moon?"

"Yeah, he's from the moon."

Upstairs, E.T. crept out of the closet. The room was
before him—a pile of clutter he'd created in his

search for transmitter parts, a search he continued now. His eyes swept the room, fine-focus on. The electrons of the room appeared, dancing their circular dance, but the inner cosmic whirl was of no help. He needed solid objects, such as—the record player. He clicked his focus back to ordinary vision and shuffled over to the machine. The turntable was empty. He put his finger on it and gave it a spin. How does a fork combine with this?

Elliott's footsteps sounded on the stair, and then the boy entered the room, carrying a tray. "Here's your supper," he said in a whisper, and handed it over. On the plate were some lettuce leaves, an apple, and an orange.

Gertie entered, pulling a little wagon filled with toys. In it she had placed a potted geranium and some other flowers, which she set at the old botanist's feet. He stared down at the offering. His heart-light fluttered. Thank you, little girl, that is very nice of you.

Michael entered, hoping that somehow the monster would have vanished, but it was there and he had to deal with it. Gertie was emptying her other gifts in front of the monster. "Here's some clay. Do you ever play with that?"

"I have an idea," said Elliott. "Where's the globe?" Michael handed it to him. Elliott turned it in front of the star-wanderer, to North America. "Look, see this is where we are . . ."

E.T. nodded. "Yeah," said Elliott, "that's where we're from. Where are you?" E.T. turned, staring out the window at the star-filled sky. He separated the

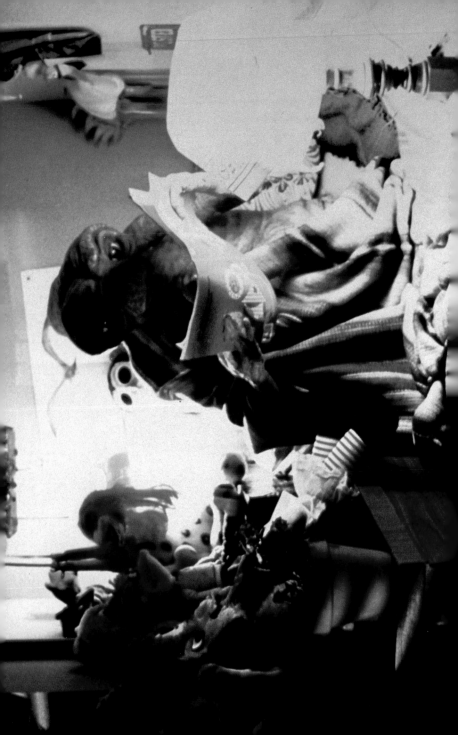

modeling clay and laid five balls down on the map of the system, around a central sun-ball.

"Five? Are you from Jupiter?"

E.T. could not understand their questioning jabber. He pointed at the five balls, and released an electron elevator from his fingertips. The balls rose up in the air and floated above the children's heads. He switched off the electron blanket and the balls fell to the floor. Then he retired into the closet with his geranium.

In the night, E.T. looked up from his pillows to see Elliott climbing out the bedroom window, onto the tiled roof. Where was the boy going?

He monitored the boy's path telepathically. Elliott was creeping onto the dread fire road, where all troubles begin. E.T. switched off his mind-radar and huddled in the closet. He reached for an Oreo cookie and chewed it nervously.

Elliott lay in the brush by the side of the fire road and watched the government agents pass, their lights sweeping in all directions. If they spotted him, he'd just say he was out walking his dog. Harvey crouched beside him, shivering nervously.

"Harvey," said Elliott quietly, "we have a great

treasure with us. Do you know that? I love him, Harvey. He's the best little guy I ever met." Elliott looked up at the stars and tried to imagine which one belonged to his new friend.

"We've got to tell, Elliott. It's too serious."

"No, he wants to stay with us." The two brothers were walking toward the school-bus stop. "Michael, listen, there are people in this neighborhood, people who've never been here before. Look at that car up there, with a man sitting in it, reading a newspaper. They're *looking* for him." Elliott's face grew tense, his voice strained. "Michael, if we turn him over to anybody else, he'll *never* get back home. I know that for sure. I feel it, like it was burned into me."

Tyler, Steve, and Greg were at the bus stop. "Say, Elliott, I forgot to ask—what ever happened to your goblin? Did he come back?" Steve asked.

"Yeah, he came back. And he wasn't a goblin. He was a spaceman," Elliott blurted out under the strain.

"What, who's a spaceman?" A small red-haired boy pushed forward, speaking in a loud, nasal voice. Lance's ratlike gaze was bright, and he seemed to sense something important was up. Elliott regretted his slip.

Gertie had no nursery school today. She was supposed to, but she'd pretended to be sick and gotten the janitor to drive her home, where she could play in peace with the monster.

She got out her wagon and started putting toys in it. Then she opened the closet door and went in. She took his hand. "Don't be scared," she said. "Elliott and I are taking care of you, so you don't have anything to worry about. Here are all my dolls in the wagon . . . and here's my rolling pin and this is my cowgirl vest. And this is my Speak and Spell. Did you ever play with one of these?"

E.T. took the bright rectangular box into his long fingers. His mind leapt suddenly into higher focus, and his heart-light fluttered.

"It teaches you to spell." She pressed a button on the box, a button marked A. The Speak and Spell spoke to Gertie. It said, quite clearly, in a man's voice, "A . . ."

"Now you watch this," said Gertie, and pressed a button marked *Go*. The box spoke, "*Spell 'mechanic.'*"

E.T. stared at the instrument, eyes flashing. Yes, it would teach him to speak an Earth language. But more important—in fact the most important of all things in the universe at that moment—it was a computer. The monster flipped the box over in his lap and removed its back. He caressed the circuits. Here was the heart of his transmitter. Computers were familiar friends. Fancy finding one that spoke! The Speak and Spell of Earth, the electronic stone by which he could master the signs and sounds of this planet. Soon he would have a complete working vocabulary. He pressed the machine's button again and again. Truly it was a friendly device, both teacher and companion. But it was more than that. It could be made to speak yet another language. It would be his own language, and he would broadcast it to the stars.

E.T.'s only error was remaining in standby telepathy with Elliott who was supposed to be cutting up a frog in biology class. Elliott began furiously covering his lab report with diagrams of highly sophisticated electronic circuitry, his hand moving as if it were writing automatically, as if controlled by a ghost. The ghost, of course, was the extraterrestrial in Elliott's closet.

Elliott wrote, right off the edge of the paper, onto the desk. His arm wrote in the air. He walked to the front of the room and began writing in chalk on the blackboard.

Tyler, Greg, and Steve stared in amazement. Tyler pointed at Elliott and made a whirling screw-loose sign with his finger near his head.

Gertie slapped a cowboy hat on E.T.'s head, to match her own cowgirl's sombrero. "Now we're both cowboys."

"B," said E.T. "B. good."

The closet door opened and Elliott entered. "Elliott," said the monster from his pillows. Elliott's mouth fell open.

"I taught him how to talk," said Gertie.

"You talked to me!" exclaimed Elliott. "E.T. Can you say that? You're E.T."

The ringing telephone interrupted their talk. *"Elliott, it's for you."*

"Hello, Elliott." Elliott felt the dangerously inquisitive probe behind Lance's voice—Lance, who never called him except to lie about how high his score had been in Asteroids. *". . . yes, Elliott, space, space, space. I seem to have it on the brain. Isn't that strange. Don't you feel something strange going on! I do . . ."*

"Hey, I gotta go . . ." Elliott hung up the phone. Lance was closing in, he could feel it. So too could E.T. who'd monitored the call. A too-curious child of that kind might—spell trouble.

And so, there was no time to lose. He pointed to the phone, and then to the window.

"Huh? Whattaya mean, E.T.?"

Again he pointed to the phone and the window. "Phone home."

"You want to—phone home?"

He nodded. "E.T. phone home."

The inside of the Speak and Spell was exposed, its guts rewired, a few strands containing traces of raspberry jam. Instead of *mechanic*, *nuisance* and other Earth words, the machine now said *doop-doople, skiggle,* and *zlock,* approximately, and much more no human ear could understand.

The boys sat beside him. He demonstrated, pressing the buttons.

"That's your language, E.T.?"

"E.T. phone home." He pointed out the window of the closet.

"And they'll come?"

He nodded. But this was only part of his transmitter, this was only his message-maker. It must be set beneath the stars and be made to run constantly, on and on, night and day, though no one be there to push its buttons. For this he needed a driving force, a thing to cause repetition, over and over. He pointed at the turntable and pantomimed putting down his own record.

"You want to make your own record?"

"Yes, yes."

"Out of what?"

"Out of—out of—" He did not know out of what. He could only describe something round, a circular shape, which he made with his hand. E.T. pointed to his own head. "Spell mechanic."

Elliott looked at the monster. "You mean, you're a mechanic."

"Yes, yes, spell mechanic." He turned the record player over and pulled out a handful of wire.

"You want more wire?"

He nodded.

To make his own rocks-and-rolling record he needed so much. His mental whirlpool was showing him the device, again and again, each time filling in another little piece. He needed . . .

He walked over to the closet, pulled out a coat and put it on. A fairly good fit, for one who had shoulders like a chicken, and of course the button was a little tight over his great cannonball of a stomach. What in the name of cosmic seas did his dressing up in a coat have to do with a beacon transmitter.

No, you old flytrap, not the coat. The coat *hanger*.

He grabbed the hanger, pointed his finger at its dowel, and burned holes in it, one for every wire connection on the Speak and Spell.

"Hey, you've got a finger like a torch, E.T."

His torch-finger quietly melted the solder on the keyboard contacts, to which he fastened what wires he had. "More . . . more . . ."

The boys brought him wire, a pie tin, a mirror, and a hubcap. He kept the wire, rejected the other objects. "Okay, E.T., we'll find you some other stuff."

He watched them depart. He must not be impatient with them.

So engrossed was he in his work, and Gertie in hers, that they didn't hear Mary climbing the stairs. They didn't hear her coming down the hall. They only heard her as she opened the door to Elliott's room.

The old monster jumped, lining himself up with the stuffed animals, goggling Muppets, and toy space robots. Mary's eyes passed over the frozen extraterrestrial lined up with the Muppets, and she didn't so much as blink.

She turned away, and he breathed a sigh of relief, which was tinged with melancholy, however. For how could she love him when he was no more to her than Kermit the Frog.

Cosmic loneliness invaded E.T.'s limbs. He tiptoed past Elliott's sleeping form, and entered the hallway. He peeked in Gertie's room, and watched for a few moments. *She* thought he was attractive, but to her, Kermit the Frog was a dashing fellow.

He crept on down the hall to Mary's room, and peeked in. The willow-creature was asleep, and he watched her for a long time. She was the loveliest creature in the universe. Gently, he placed an M&M on her pillow and crept back down the hall. Harvey the dog was waiting.

They continued on their nightly prowl into the kitchen.

E.T. pointed. "Re-frigg-er-a-tor." He opened the door and took out milk and a Pepperidge Farm chocolate cake. Harvey whined pathetically and E.T. presented him with a leftover pork chop.

Harvey gazed up at E.T. I'm *your* dog. If any trouble comes around, let me know.

A van filled with audio-snooping devices sensitive enough to impress even an intergalactic traveler appeared on the block. And the operator at the illuminated control panel had a large ring of keys at his belt. Floating in upon Keys were voices from the neighborhood:

"*Mom, to make cookies, is a cup of milk the same as a cup of flour?*"

And: "*I'll be baby-sitting tonight, Jack, if you want to come over . . .*"

And: "*His communicator is finished, Michael. We can take it out and set it up.*"

The man with the keys waved his hand and the van came to a stop.

"*You know, Elliott, he's not looking too good lately.*"

"*Don't say that, Michael. We're fine!*"

"*What's this 'we' stuff? You say 'we' all the time now.*"

"*It's his telepathy. I'm—so close to him, I feel like I am him.*"

To the ordinary snooper, this conversation would have been passed over; to Keys it was as potent as a signal from Mars. The street map was brought out, and Mary's house marked with a large red circle.

Elliott explained Halloween to E.T. as best he could, pointing out that this would be E.T.'s only chance to walk around the neighborhood in plain view. ". . . because *everybody* will be looking weird. See? Hey, I'm sorry, E.T., I didn't mean that *you* were weird—just different."

Elliott put a sheet over the old voyager's head, and huge, furry bedroom slippers over his paddles. "Looks good," said Elliott. "We could take you anywhere."

Downstairs, Mary looked at him and said, "Gertie, that's a wonderful costume. How did you get your stomach so fat?" She patted the great pumpkin shape.

"We padded it with pillows," said Elliott nervously, dragging E.T. away and out to the garage where Gertie was waiting in her sheet. And so was his beacon transmitter—umbrella folded, other components closed in a cardboard box.

"Okay, E.T., hop on." They lifted him into the basket of the bike, attached his communicator to the carrying rack over the rear wheel, and pushed off down the driveway, into the street. Earth children walked along the street: princesses, cats, clowns, hoboes, pirates, devils, gorillas, vampires, and Frankensteins. Earth was truly an amazing place.

"Why, that's the most incredible costume I've ever seen," said the man in the hallway. E.T. had removed his sheet. In his cowboy hat and bedroom slippers, with his incredible eyes, stomach on the floor, and feet like a toadshade plant, he was certainly in a class by himself. Every house they'd gone to had been like this, with a big fuss made over him. He liked it. He'd been in a closet for weeks. Now he held out his trick-or-treat basket and received a great deal of candy.

They moved from neighborhood to neighborhood. "Okay," said Elliott, "let's try that house over there." But as the door opened, E.T.'s eyes clicked in fear, for there was a red-haired little nerd he knew at once had to be Lance, about whom he'd always been suspicious.

"Who's *this?*" Lance asked.

"It's—it's my cousin," stammered Elliott.

"He's plenty weird," said Lance, taking a step closer. E.T. backed up, Elliott backing with him. They hopped on the bike and E.T. said, "Spell *fast,*" as Elliott pumped for all he was worth.

What would Lance do? Go to the authorities? Elliott looked over his shoulder but could not see Lance. He steered his bike off the highway, onto the fire road, and pedaled up it. Now that they were close to the landing site, E.T.'s mind was racing. He must set up his communicator, and begin signaling.

"Elliott—"

"Yeah?"

"Spell *hang on.*" E.T. moved his fingers, releasing a low-level anti-gravity formula, and the bicycle lifted off the ground. It skimmed the bushes, then the treetops, and sailed on over the forest.

When they reached the clearing, E.T. controlled the descent and the bicycle slipped in over the grass and touched gently down.

Elliott began unpacking the communicator. E.T. signaled that they should begin setting up the transmitter.

. . . *geeple   doople   zwak-zwak   snafn   olg mnnnnin* . . .

Elliott stood in the flow of the signal, hoping for its success, but it seemed so small, such a feeble thing searching up there in the immensity. The extraterrestrial, seeing his doubts, touched the boy's shoulder. "We have found a window."

"We have?"

"Our frequency is that window. It will reach Them."

They stood with their transmitter for a long time, both of them silent. The stars seemed to listen too—and of course, the nerd in the bushes was listening.

Mary walked toward the insistent doorbell and opened the door.

". . . investigating rumors of unidentified flying objects . . ."

She stared at the ring of keys hanging from his belt. Then he showed her what appeared to be a government badge.

"I'm sorry," she stammered, "but I don't understand . . ."

"Not far from here, a UFO put down. We have reason to believe one of its crew was stranded . . ."

"You've got to be kidding."

"I assure you—" his eyes penetrated her own. "—I'm not."

The geranium was drooping, as was E.T., head down, hands folded like a pair of dead squid in his lap. All hope for his communicator had left him. It had been running for weeks, and there was no answer from space. The crew of the Great Ship was far off, speeding fast, gone beyond recalling.

I'm dying, Master, whispered the geranium faintly, but the old botanist could do nothing; the plant was absorbing his emotions, and over those he had no control. Cosmic loneliness had gotten to the marrow of his bones.

When Elliott came home, horror crossed his face as he looked at the color of E.T.'s face. It was a grayish shade which drew his gaze hypnotically into warps of dreaming he wasn't up to, at all. He sank down, grabbing the old hand in his own.

Elliott brought in every medicine the family cupboard held, but they just lay in his room like toy medicines, useless for what ailed the creature in the bed. Every plant in the house was dead. The walls themselves seemed to be heaving toward him, with each breath of his own lung.

"Heal yourself," begged Elliott, for he felt the old genius could do anything. E.T. slowly shook his head.

"Carry me . . . far away . . ." whispered E.T. ". . . and leave me . . ."

"E.T.," said Elliott. "I'd never leave you."

The lost voyager summoned himself back toward

the surface again, to speak, to plead. "I am . . . a grave danger to you . . ." He lifted the tip of his finger. ". . . and to your planet . . ." He lifted his head, his star-eyes shining in the moonlight.

"But our communicator," said Elliott. "It's still working."

"Junk," said E.T. His eyes flashed in the darkness.

"You're not even trying," said Elliott, afraid of the eyes, and drawn to them. "Please, E.T."

The night passed on. E.T.'s body became more rigid, and gray all over. Elliott's body felt as though it were made of chains, chains of iron holding him down. He felt heavier and heavier; his head was splitting, and dark depression weighed on him like a hundred thousand tons of lead. When the gray light of morning finally came, he pulled himself up and looked at E.T. The monster was like something drained, no longer gray, but white, a white dwarf.

Elliott dragged himself into the hallway, and staggered down it to Mary's room. She looked at him and said, "What's wrong?"

"Everything—is worth nothing," he said, feeling the deep in-falling, the collapsing, the departing.

"Oh, baby, that's no way to feel," said Mary, though in fact it was exactly how she felt too; all night she'd been dreaming she was underwater, unable to get to the surface.

"I have something wonderful," said Elliott, "and I've made it sad."

"Everyone feels like that now and then," said Mary. She patted the bed, indicating the space beside her. Warmth was better than words.

What was going on in the house? She sensed that there was something at its core, unnameable, horrible, gathering everything to it.

"Can you . . . tell me about it?" she asked.

"Later . . ." Elliott snuggled against her.

"Go to sleep," said Mary, stroking his brow. "Go to sleep."

The next morning while Mary fixed breakfast, Michael tried to wake Elliott. He came around slowly, but Michael felt like he was dragging an iron ball as he helped Elliott down the hall to his room. What had happened to his brother? What had happened to the house? Was it caving in or something?

He dragged Elliott into the bedroom where E.T. was stretched out under a blanket, turning as white as ash.

"We've got to tell now, Elliott," said Michael. "We need help."

"No, you can't, Michael. Don't . . ." Elliott knew the rest of the world must not come in on them. They'd seize the miraculous creature and do things to him.

"Elliott," Michael pleaded, "we'll lose him if we don't get help. And Elliott, we'll lose you . . ."

Elliott was glowing like iron in a furnace. He could always fake a fever, but this . . .

Michael grabbed Elliott under one arm and lifted E.T. with the other. He dragged them into the bathroom and dumped them in the shower. He had to put out this fire, had to cool Elliott down . . .

The water came on, soaking Elliott and E.T. Michael went downstairs to get Mary. "Mom, I have something to tell you." He led her upstairs to the bathroom with Gertie following. Michael pulled the shower curtain back. Mary blinked and her eyes remained closed for one hesitant second. Then she saw Elliott and—

"He's from the moon," said Gertie.

Mary grabbed Elliott and dragged him from the shower. "Downstairs, all of you," she said, wrapping Elliott in a towel and pushing them ahead of her. Her mind wasn't working rationally. The thing in the shower could stay there. She was getting out with the kids.

She opened the front door and there was an astronaut on the doorstep. She slammed the door in his face and bolted for a window. A sheet of plastic came over it and she watched a man in a spacesuit taping it to the frame.

Then, moments later, an enormous plastic envelope came down, enclosing the entire house.

By nightfall the house had been converted into a gigantic airtight package, draped in transparent vinyl, with huge air hoses climbing up over the roof and circling the structure. Bright lights, braced on tall scaffolding, illuminated it on all sides. The street was blocked off, and trailers and trucks were parked in the drive. Men came and went in blue jumpsuits.

Entry to the house was through a van. Keys was in the van, putting on his jumpsuit and helmet. He opened the back door of the van and stepped into one of the enormous hoses. He walked along through it to a pneumatic seal, he unzipped it and entered the quarantined house.

A team of doctors worked over Mary and the children while others hovered around E.T. prodding, poking, X-raying, sticking needles and thermometers into him.

"Apparently, the children were able to establish a primitive language system with the creature. Seven, eight, monosyllabic words," a doctor said.

"*I* taught him to talk," Gertie told the doctor.

"You taught him to talk?"

"With my Speak and Spell."

"Have you seen your friend exhibit any emotions? Has he laughed or cried?"

"He cried," said Gertie. "He wanted to go home."

Keys unzipped a plastic door and entered another room where the quarantine had been most completely imposed. The entire room was draped in plastic, and within it was still another room, ten feet by ten, plastic and transparent. Inside were Elliott and E.T., a team of medical specialists working around them.

"Sonar, have you got a location on the creature's heart?"

"Difficult to see."

"Well, does it *have* a heart?"

"The entire screen is lit up. It looks like his whole chest is . . . a heart."

A needle punctured E.T.'s skin. On the table beside him, Elliott winced, as if the puncture had entered his own body. He turned toward Keys. "You're hurting him. You're killing us . . ."

Keys stared down at E.T. The vision he'd had of a noble space creature had altered radically in the face of E.T.'s ugliness. But this thing on the table before him, ugly as it was, was from the Ship, and the Ship was infinite in its sweep and power. And he wanted that Ship.

"We're trying to help him, Elliott. He's sick. He needs attention."

"He wants to stay with me. He doesn't know you."

"Elliott, your friend is a rare and valuable creature. We want to know him. If we can get to know him, we can learn so many things about the universe and about life. You saved him and were good to him. Can't you let us do our part now? Wherever he goes, you'll go . . . I promise you that."

But where the creature was going, none could follow. The whirling powers of his body were shifting again at the core. The old being felt the enormity of this power. Was he to destroy this planet? No, he cried to himself, it must not come to that. What more horrible fate could there be than to destroy a thing so lovely as Earth? E.T. clung to the edge of the void, on a last thin thread of energy.

"The boy's unconscious again."

"I'm losing blood pressure . . . and pulse . . . increase oxygen . . . zap him!"

An electric device was applied to E.T.'s chest, but the EKG reading was a solid steady line, heart action ceased. E.T. lay dead—but Elliott stirred, all of his strength returning almost at the moment E.T.'s heart had stopped.

E.T. had found at least one of the formulas he sought, that of a shield, cast behind him as he swooned into death, so the boy could not follow.

Elliott jerked upright in bed, screaming, "E.T., don't go!"

The clean-room was cleared of everyone, including Elliott, who stood outside it, staring in as E.T. was zipped into a plastic bag and covered with dry ice. A small lead coffin was brought in, and agents placed the extraterrestrial in the box.

Tears spilled down Elliott's face. "I thought I'd get to keep you forever. And I had a million things to show you, E.T. You were like a wish come true. But it wasn't a wish I knew I had till you came to me. Have you gone someplace else now?"

Geeple geeple snnnnnnnnnnnn org

A beam of golden light shot through inner space. It touched E.T.'s healing finger and caused it to glow. He healed himself. He did not know how. A brilliant glow filled his entire body and he felt golden all over, but especially in his heart-light.

Elliott noticed it, unzipped the bag and scraped away the ice from E.T.'s chest and saw the glow. He turned toward the door where Keys was talking to Mary. He quickly covered the heart-light with his hands.

E.T.'s eyes opened. "E.T. phone home."

"*Okay!*" said Elliott in a joyful whisper.

Elliott laid the dry ice back in over E.T. and zipped the bag closed. Then he went out, face in his hands, pushing past Mary and Keys. He found Michael and whispered to him. Michael made one quiet phone call and slipped out the side door.

Elliott was standing at the main air tube leading from the house as the agents came by carrying the lead box. They carried the coffin through the hose, deposited it in the van, and returned.

"I'm going with E.T.," Elliott said.

Keys sighed, pulled the zipper door back, and let Elliott through. He scrambled up into the van and knocked on the door to the cab. Michael, in the driver's seat turned. "Elliott, there's just one thing. I've only backed Mom's car out of the driveway. I've never driven forward before."

Then he put the van in gear, stepped on the gas, and pulled away. A horrible ripping sound signaled that the entire hose system was tearing from the house. The van skidded to the bottom of the drive, trailing 20 feet of main hose behind it. Michael leaned on the horn, and policemen scurried to move the sawhorses, and the crowd parted to let the van through.

Mary jumped into her car with Gertie and squealed around the corner after the van. She knew now that the monster was alive and whether wishes or just dumb luck had brought it back to life, she was glad. It was causing complications because police cars were chasing her, but she knew that somehow —it was the best.

The van streaked to a stop, and Elliott and Michael helped E.T. down. The Dungeoners—Greg, Tyler, and Steve—stood open-mouthed as the little monster was brought toward them.

"He's a man from outer space," said Elliott, "and we're taking him to his Ship."

Feeling as if their minds had just fallen apart, the boys nevertheless helped E.T. into Elliott's bicycle basket and raced off. Tyler led, long legs pumping up and down on his pedals. A glance back over his shoulder gave him another mind-boggling view of the thing in Elliott's basket, and he pumped faster, eager to get rid of it in a hurry, whatever it was. Before it started multiplying.

As this strange crew of cyclists dipped out of sight, the hilltop filled again with government vehicles, police cars, and Mary. They all screeched to a stop and threw open the door to the van. But there was nothing inside except some dry ice which spilled out at them.

At that moment a figure ran out of the bushes yelling. "They took their bikes! I know where they're going!" It was Lance. "The lake, they're headed for the far side of the lake."

The police sailed off with the agents in the direction of the lake.

Lance turned to Mary. "The forest—I'll show you."

"But—the lake?"

"Hey, I may be a nerd, but I'm not stupid, you know."

E.T. and company pedaled on toward the landing site. E.T. bounced in Elliott's basket, hanging onto it with his long fingers. His head was buzzing with signals, buzzing with *znackle nerk nerk znackle do you read us?*

Yes, my captain. But please hurry will you *zinggg zingle nerk nerk*

"They're coming!" Michael glanced toward Elliott. The police cars had circled the lake and found nothing. Then they had picked up on E.T.'s signal, searching the heavens with a telepathic probe so strong that even the stones could feel it.

The bikes bounced and swerved over the cracks and slim rubber tires screeched as they skimmed over the asphalt. They reached the last piece of street in their path, the last city block before the forest, before escape. Suddenly it was filled with agents on both ends and cops in the middle.

Tyler crouched over his ten-speed. He pedaled forward, Michael beside him, and Elliott right behind, bikes revved as fast as they could go. The phalanx of bikes drove toward the wall of police and government agents. All the corridors were blocked.

One last crash, thought Elliott. That's all we could give him. But E.T. raised a finger and gave a little lift to the chase. The bikes shot into the air over the tops of the pursuit cars. Five bikes were sailing over the houses. E.T. gazed down at the ground below. Yes, this was much better, a smoother ride. His heart-light had come on again, and was shining through Elliott's bicycle basket.

Mary maneuvered her car up the same hillside, instructed by Lance. The greatest bike chase of all time and he wasn't in on it.

Above the treetops, Elliott led his party swiftly to the hidden communicator. "There . . ." E.T. pointed with his finger.

Ullll-leeple-leep

The communicator hummed. As Elliott approached it, a sudden beam of brilliant lavender light broke over him. He froze and looked at E.T., who stepped into the light with him, and together they looked up.

The Great Ship was overhead, soft lights glowing. Elliott stared at the beautiful vehicle, drinking in the greatness of its power. It was E.T. multiplied a millionfold, the greatest heart-light the world had ever seen. He turned toward E.T.

E.T.'s eyes had grown bigger, too, filling with the sight of the beloved mother ship, Queen of the Milky Way. He looked at his friend who had helped him to call across an incalculable distance. "Thank you, Elliott . . ." His voice had become stronger already . . .

At that moment he saw the willow-creature enter the clearing, and he gazed at her in silence. Gertie ran toward him. "Here's your flower," she said, holding out the geranium. He lifted her into his arms. "B. Good."

A shadow moved at the edge of the clearing, and the sound of jingling keys filled the night. E.T. quickly set Gertie down. He turned to Elliott and held out his hand. "Come?"

"Stay," Elliott said.

E.T. embraced the boy, and felt the cosmic loneliness run through him as deep as any he'd ever felt. He touched Elliott's forehead. "I'll be right here," he said, fingertip glowing.

Then he walked up the gangplank. The inner light of the Great Gem glowed above him, and he felt the millionfold circuits of its awareness lighting in him until his heart, like Elliott's, had filled not with loneliness but with love.

He went into the misty light, with his geranium.